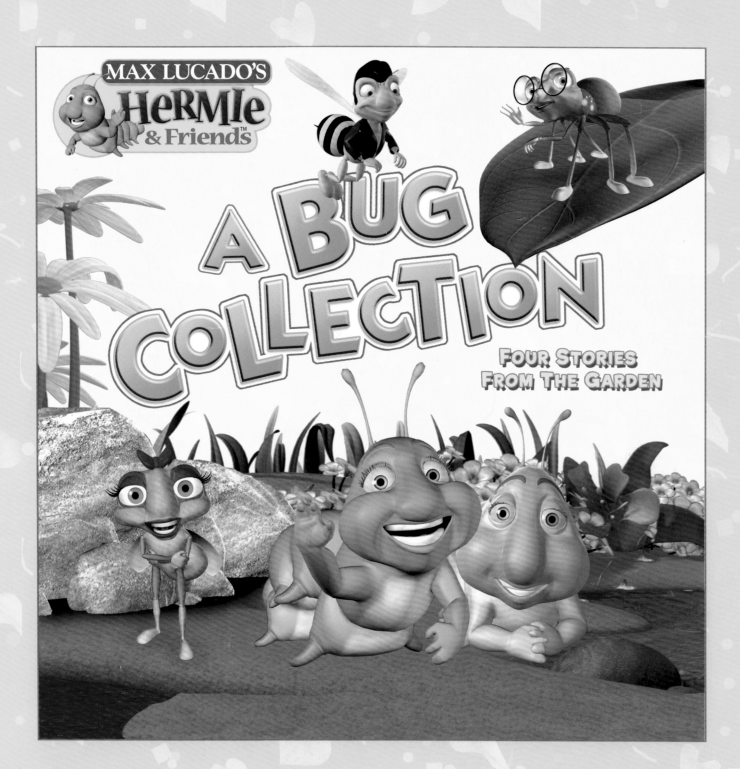

MAX LUCADO'S
HeRMIe
& Friends™

A BUG COLLECTION

FOUR STORIES
FROM THE GARDEN

A Bug Collection: Four Stories from the Garden

Hermie, A Common Caterpillar
Text and art copyright © 2002 by Max Lucado.
Illustrations by GlueWorks Animation.

Flo, The Lyin' Fly
Text and art copyright © 2004 by Max Lucado.
Story by Troy Schmidt, based on the characters from Max Lucado's *Hermie: A Common Caterpillar*.
Illustrations by GlueWorks Animation.

Webster, The Scaredy Spider
Text and art copyright © 2004 by Max Lucado.
Story by Troy Schmidt, based on the characters from Max Lucado's *Hermie: A Common Caterpillar*.
Illustrations by GlueWorks Animation.

Buzby, The Misbehaving Bee
Text and art copyright © 2005 by Max Lucado.
Story by Troy Schmidt, based on the characters from Max Lucado's *Hermie: A Common Caterpillar*.
Illustrations by GlueWorks Animation.

Published in Nashville, Tennessee. Thomas Nelson is a trademark of Thomas Nelson, Inc.

Thomas Nelson, Inc. titles may be purchased in bulk for educational, business, fundraising, or sales promotional use. For information, please email SpecialMarkets@ThomasNelson.com.

ISBN 10: 1-4003-1049-0
ISBN 13: 978-1-4003-1049-4

Printed in China
07 08 09 10 11 MULTI 9 8 7 6 5 4 3 2 1

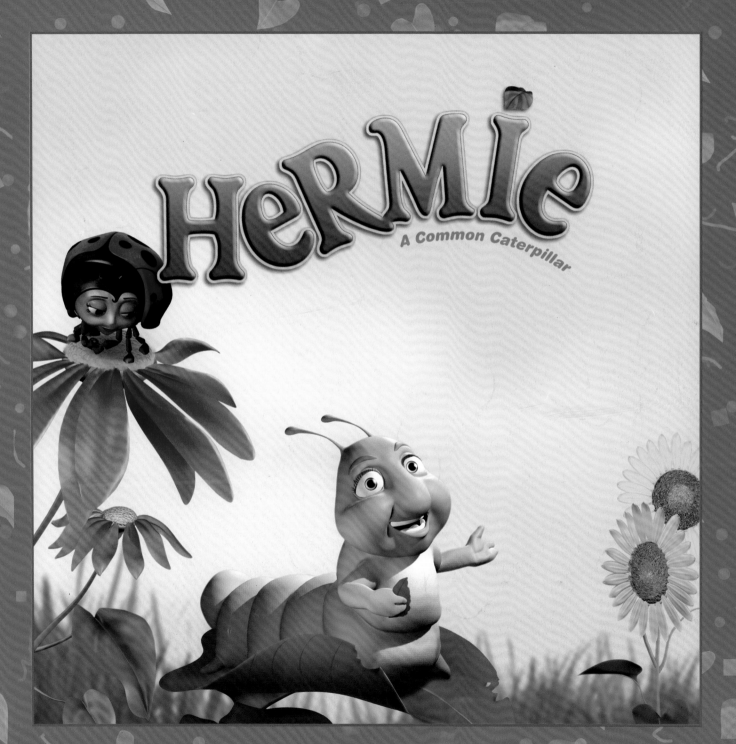

Hermie was a common caterpillar.

Now, as a rule, caterpillars aren't very exciting. But Hermie was even more ordinary than most.

He didn't have stripes, and he didn't have spots.

He had nothing but smooth green skin and a bunch of feet.

He ate common leaves and squirmed through common grass.

Hermie was just a common caterpillar.

But Hermie did one thing that wasn't common. He talked to God. Hermie and his friend Wormie would ask God, "Why did You make us so common? Other caterpillars have stripes. Some have spots."

God would answer, "I love you, Hermie and Wormie. But I'm not finished with you yet. I'm giving you a heart like Mine."

So they felt better . . . until they met Antonio Ant carrying a big pine cone.

Antonio Ant was smaller than either of them, but on his shoulder was a big pine cone. Hermie and Wormie were amazed at Antonio's strength.

"Wow!" Wormie said. "How do you carry such a heavy load?"

"God made me strong," replied Antonio.

Hermie and Wormie felt sad. They asked God, "Why can't we be strong like the ant?"

God's answer was kind. "I love you just the way you are. But I'm not finished with you yet."

So they felt better . . . until one rainy day when they saw Schneider Snail.

"You need a house like I have," said Schneider.

"That's your *house*?" Wormie asked.

"It sure is. Watch." And with that . . . Schneider pulled his head into his shell. "See, it's nice and dry in here."

Hermie and Wormie wondered why God hadn't given *them* a cozy house like the snail's.

God reminded them, "Be patient, Hermie and Wormie. I'm not finished with you yet."

That made Hermie and
Wormie feel much better . . .
until they saw Lucy Ladybug.

"You have such pretty spots!"
Hermie exclaimed.

"Beautiful!" Wormie agreed.

"You are very kind," Lucy replied softly.
"But I had nothing to do with it. This is the
way God made me."

Hermie and Wormie wanted to be grateful
for the gift God had given the ladybug, but it
was hard. Both of them felt so . . . common.

That night, underneath the bright stars, Henrie prayed. "We're sorry, God. We know you love us, but we don't understand why You made us so . . ."

"Common?" God finished the sentence.

"Yes, common," both caterpillars said at the same time.

"Remember," God told them. "I love you just the way you are, but I'm not finished with you yet. I'm giving you a heart like Mine."

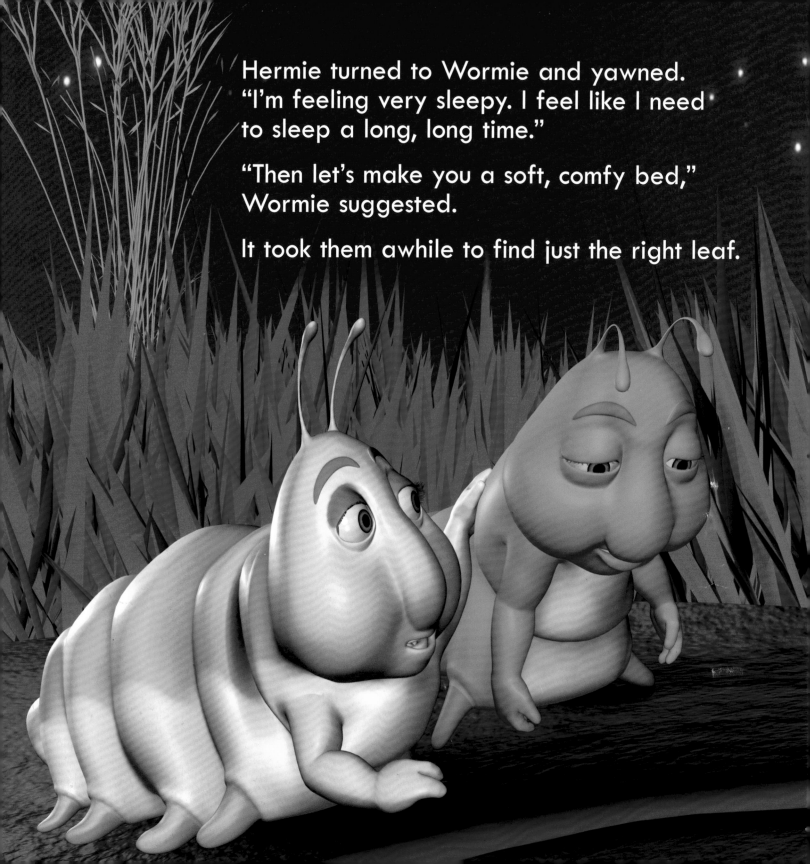

Hermie turned to Wormie and yawned. "I'm feeling very sleepy. I feel like I need to sleep a long, long time."

"Then let's make you a soft, comfy bed," Wormie suggested.

It took them awhile to find just the right leaf.

"There," Wormie said to his friend. "Have a good, long rest. I'll be waiting for you when you wake up."

Hermie thanked his friend. Then he prayed to God and said, "You know, God, it's okay that I'm just a common caterpillar. You love me, and *that* makes me special."

Hermie snuggled into his bed, closed his eyes, and drifted off to sleep.

As Hermie slept, he dreamed that he was different.

He had strength like the ant.

He had a house like the snail.

He had spots like the ladybug.

He dreamed that he was no longer a common caterpillar but that he had something special.

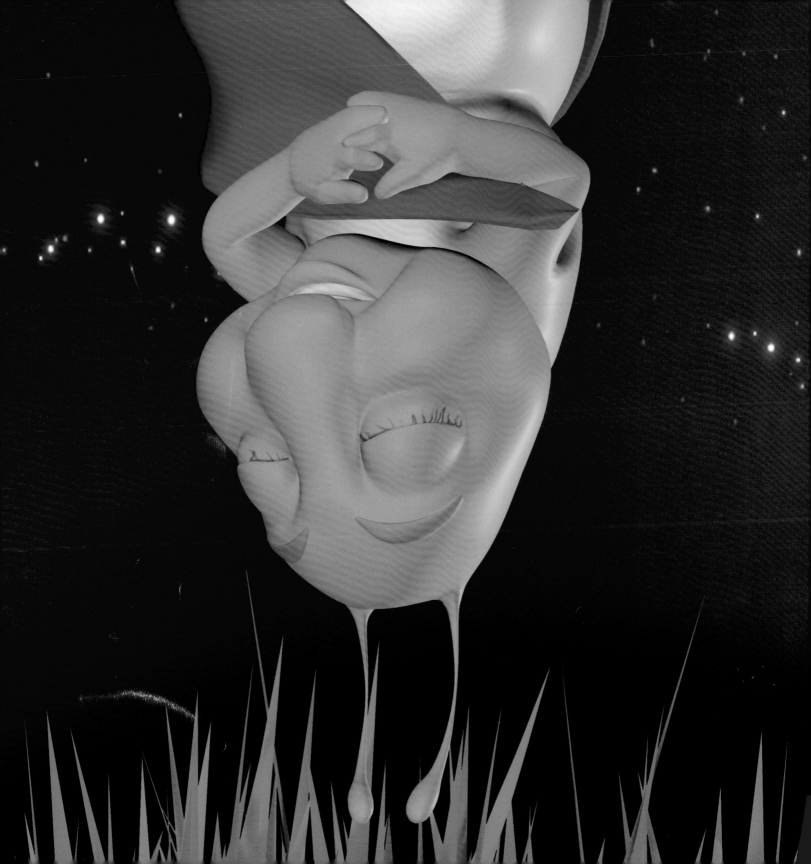

After what seemed to be a long time, Hermie woke up. It was dark, and he was covered from head to toe.

What had happened to his comfy bed? He wiggled and squirmed to get out, and when he did . . .

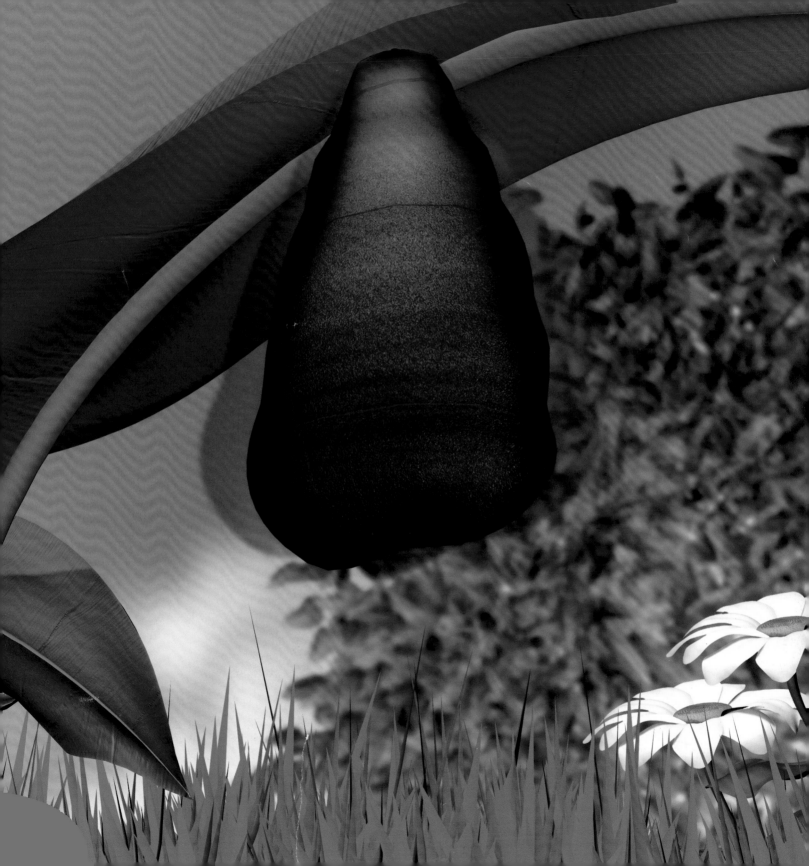

. . . he and his bed began to fall down, down . . .

. . . until, suddenly his bed cracked open, and Hermie felt a tickle on his back.

Then, something wonderful happened!

Wings fluttered open—wings he didn't even know he had!

They were glorious, wide, brightly colored wings with beautiful spots . . . and they were *his*.

With hardly any effort, Hermie began to fly. Up and up, higher and higher, he soared over the trees.

That's when Hermie realized what God had done. Now he understood.

God had made Hermie special—inside and out.

He wasn't like the ant . . . or the snail . . . or the ladybug. He was Hermie—a beautiful butterfly with a beautiful heart.

Hermie had to tell Wormie the good news.

"Wormie!" came a voice from high in the sky.

"Hermie, where are you?" Wormie asked.

"I'm up here!"

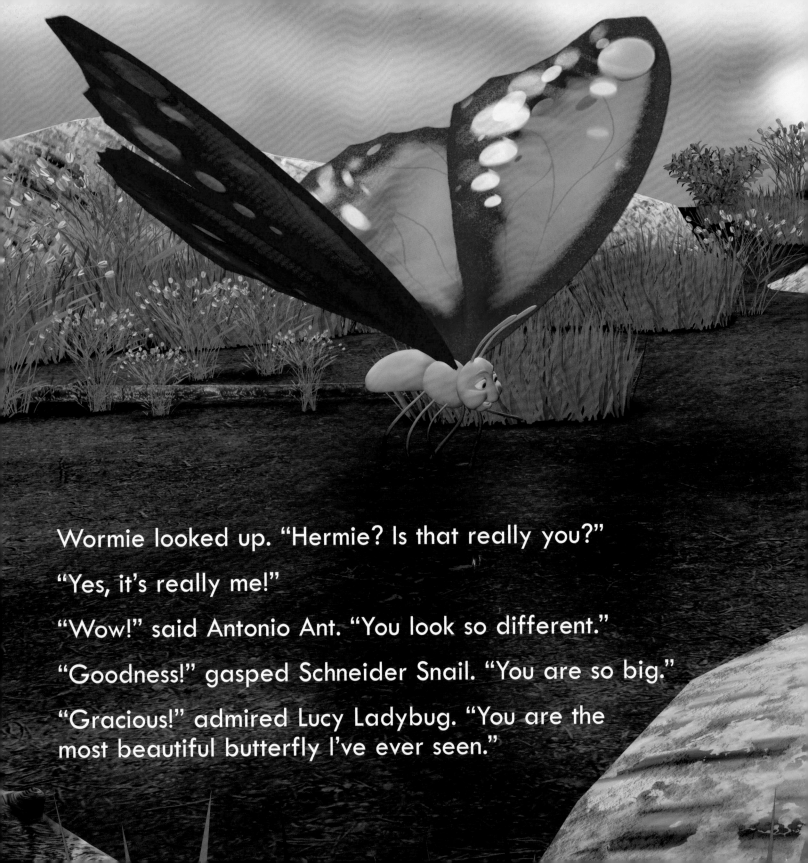

Wormie looked up. "Hermie? Is that really you?"

"Yes, it's really me!"

"Wow!" said Antonio Ant. "You look so different."

"Goodness!" gasped Schneider Snail. "You are so big."

"Gracious!" admired Lucy Ladybug. "You are the most beautiful butterfly I've ever seen."

"God was not finished with me after all!" Hermie announced. Then he flew down and stopped right next to Wormie.

He gave a big butterfly grin and whispered. "Wormie, God loves you just the way you are. But, guess what? God is not finished with you, either."

Wormie's smile grew bigger and bigger. Now he understood, too.

"You know? You may be right. I'm starting to feel pretty sleepy, too." Wormie yawned a big yawn. Hermie smiled a big smile.

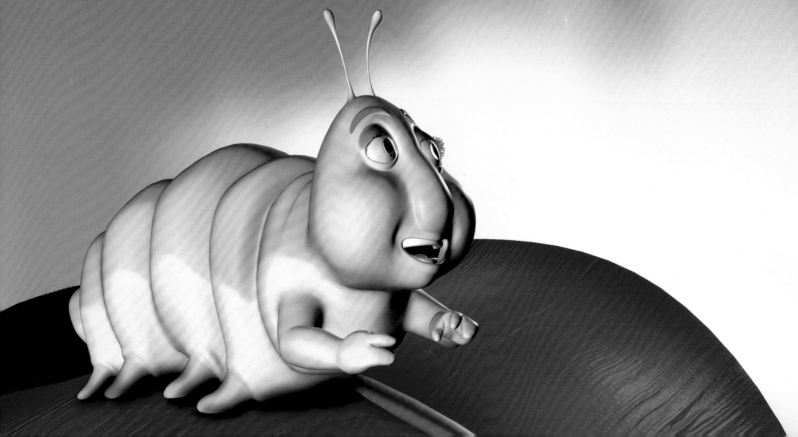

FLO
The Lyin' Fly

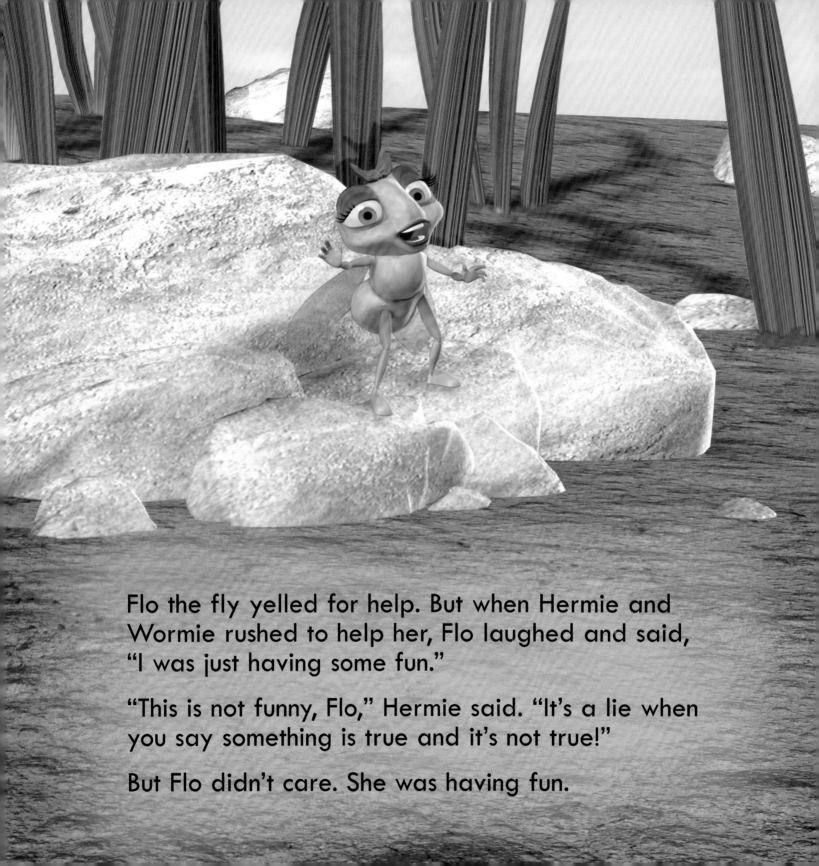

Flo the fly yelled for help. But when Hermie and Wormie rushed to help her, Flo laughed and said, "I was just having some fun."

"This is not funny, Flo," Hermie said. "It's a lie when you say something is true and it's not true!"

But Flo didn't care. She was having fun.

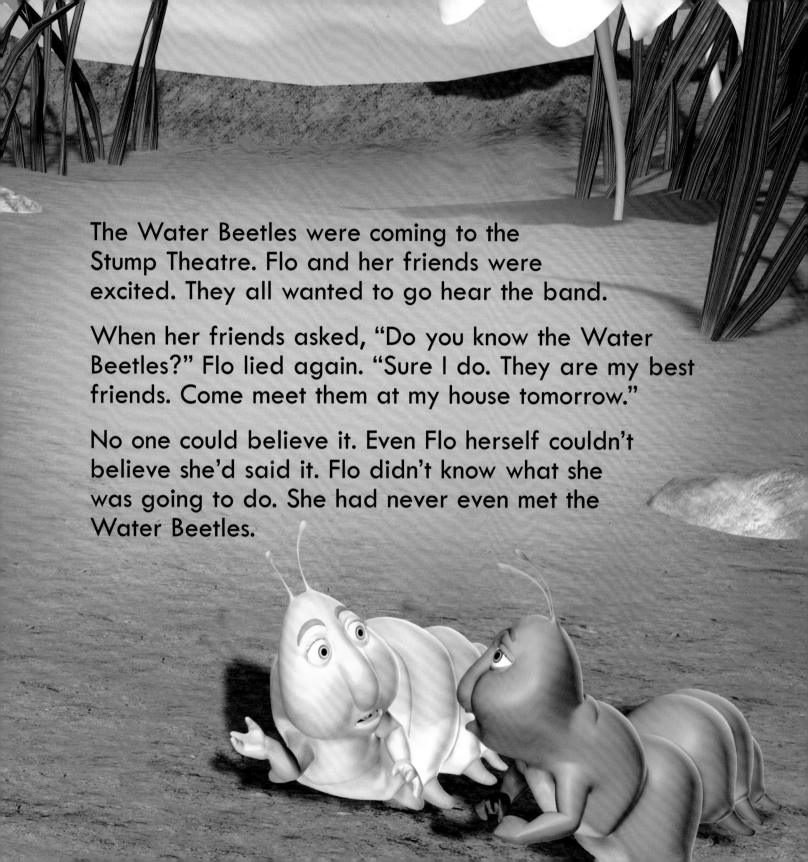

The Water Beetles were coming to the Stump Theatre. Flo and her friends were excited. They all wanted to go hear the band.

When her friends asked, "Do you know the Water Beetles?" Flo lied again. "Sure I do. They are my best friends. Come meet them at my house tomorrow."

No one could believe it. Even Flo herself couldn't believe she'd said it. Flo didn't know what she was going to do. She had never even met the Water Beetles.

The next morning, Flo tried to make sticks and acorns look like the Water Beetles, but it didn't work. One of the Beetles fell down.

Bailey, one of the ladybug twins, pointed at Flo. "You don't know the Water Beetles! You lied."

Caitlin Caterpillar led the group away. "C'mon, girls, I'm not listening to these lies anymore."

Flo's friends left, and she was all alone.

Flo prayed, "God, my friends don't like me."

"Flo, they don't trust you because you lied," God said. "To gain back their trust, be like Me," God said. "When I make a promise, I keep it. When I say something, I mean it. You can do the same."

"Will you help me?" Flo asked.

"I will," God answered.

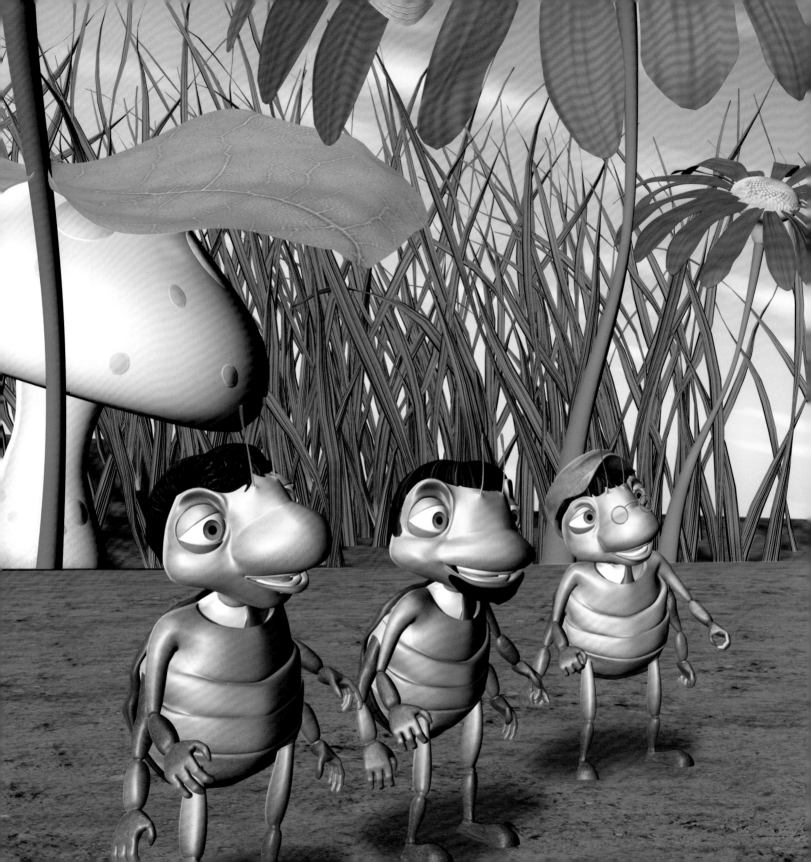

Suddenly, Flo heard a voice behind her. "Excuse me."

Flo turned around. She could not believe her eyes. "The Water Beetles!" Flo screamed.

"We need to get to the concert tonight. Can you help us?"

"Yes, I can!" said Flo, "First come to my house and have some mango nectar."

While the Water Beetles rested at Flo's, she zipped off to tell her friends the news.

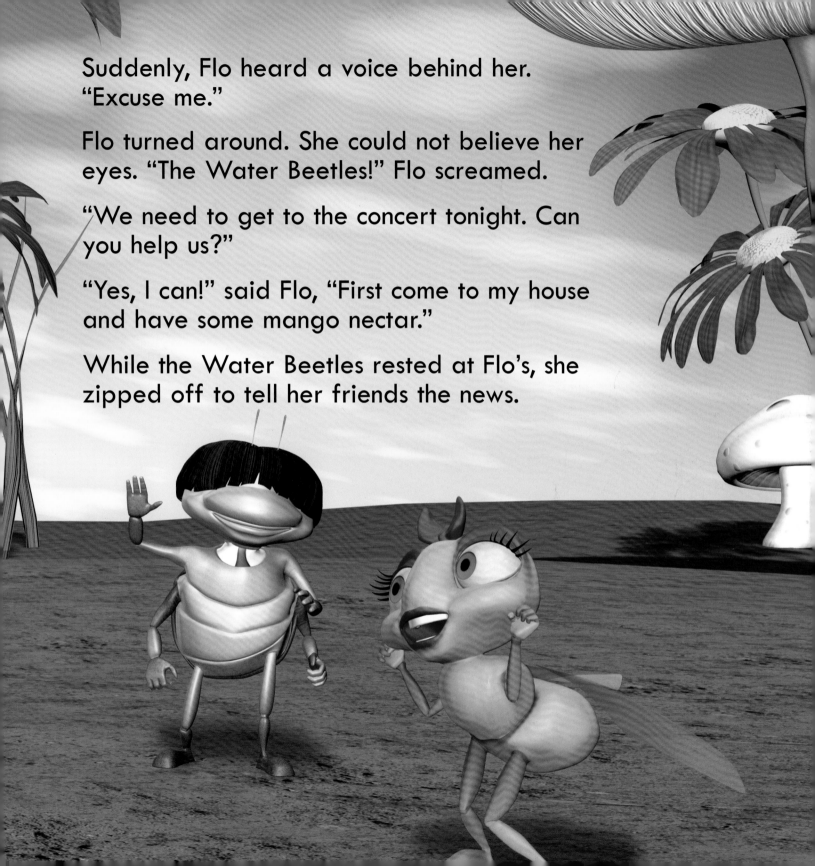

Flo found Hermie and Wormie.

"You won't believe it," Flo said. "The Water Beetles got lost, and they're at my house. I really met them!"

Hermie and Wormie said nothing. They were sad for Flo and all her lies.

Flo flew away. "Nobody believes me," she cried. "It's all because of the lies I told."

What Flo didn't know was that someone was watching her . . . someone very mysterious. And he believed her story.

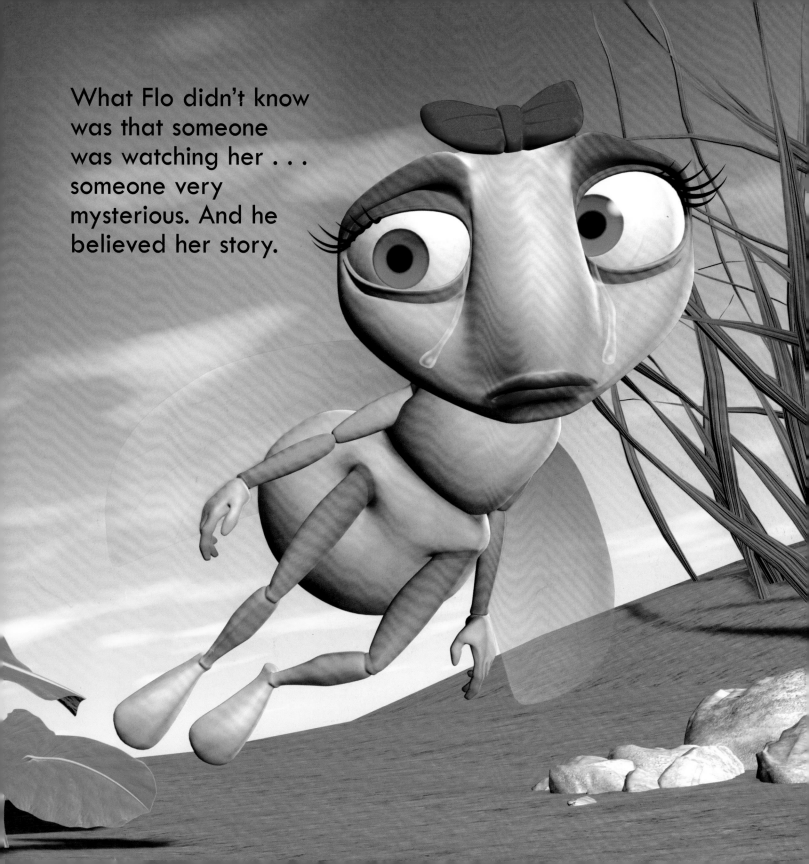

That night, Flo and the Water Beetles headed to the concert. Suddenly, Puffy the dragonfly swooped down, scooped up the band, and took them to his home at the top of a very tall tree.

"Oh, no! Heeeellppppp! Heeeellppppp!" Flo screamed. But no one came.

Quickly, Flo flew to the concert, rushed onto the stage, and grabbed the microphone. Standing before all the fans, she yelled, "Heeeellllppppp! Heeeellllppppp! The Water Beetles have been kidnapped!"

The crowd looked up, but no one believed Flo because of all the lies she had told.

She would have to help the Water Beetles all by herself.

Flo flew to Puffy's home where she found
the Water Beetles and Puffy inside.

"What's going on here?" Flo asked.

"They said they'd sing a song." Puffy frowned.

"But we're late for the concert," Flo said. "We have to go."

Puffy glared at the Water Beetles and stood in their way.
"I said . . . NOW!"

The Water Beetles started to sing. Puffy
was so busy listening, he didn't even notice
Flo tying a stick to his tail.

At just the right time, Flo yelled, "RUN!"

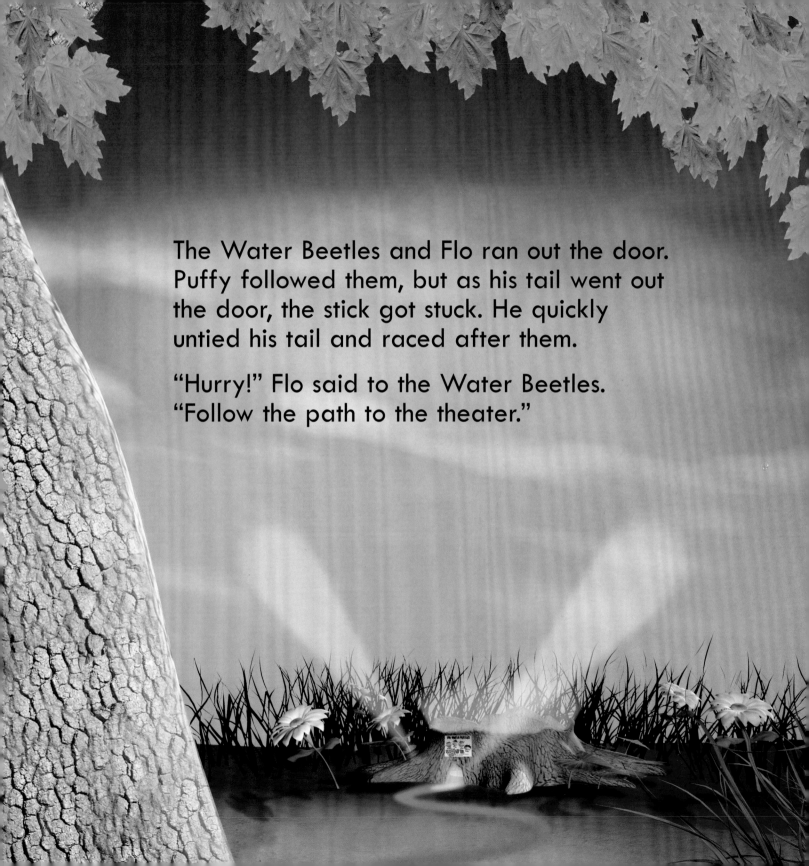

The Water Beetles and Flo ran out the door. Puffy followed them, but as his tail went out the door, the stick got stuck. He quickly untied his tail and raced after them.

"Hurry!" Flo said to the Water Beetles. "Follow the path to the theater."

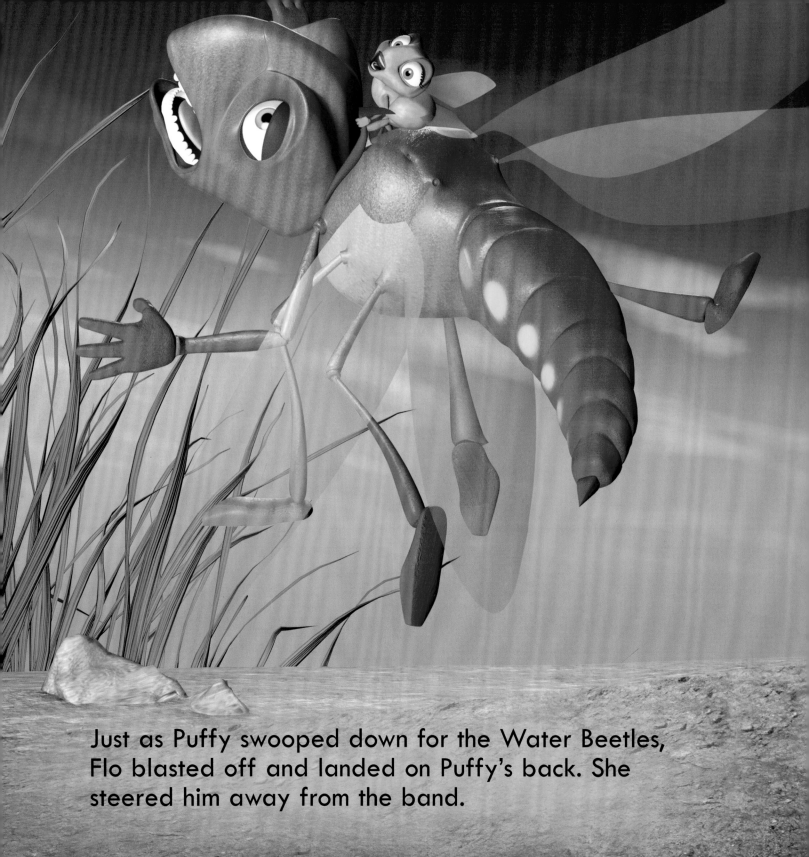

Just as Puffy swooped down for the Water Beetles, Flo blasted off and landed on Puffy's back. She steered him away from the band.

"You won't mess with my friends!" Flo yelled. The Water Beetles stopped and watched Flo and Puffy fly off into the distance, disappearing over the horizon.

The Water Beetles made their way toward the concert, their heads hung low. Their friend was gone.

At the concert, the Water Beetles walked onto the stage. Everyone yelled and screamed, but the Water Beetles seemed sad and upset. Slowly the noise faded and they began to speak.

"Bugs and buggettes, something terrible happened tonight. We were kidnapped." The crowd gasped.

They told the whole story, just as Flo had told it.

The crowd could not believe it. Flo had told the truth and nobody believed her—not even her best friends.

Suddenly, down from the sky flew Puffy—
and Flo! Flo was riding on the back of a tired
and dazed Puffy. The crowd applauded as
Flo and Puffy landed on the stage.

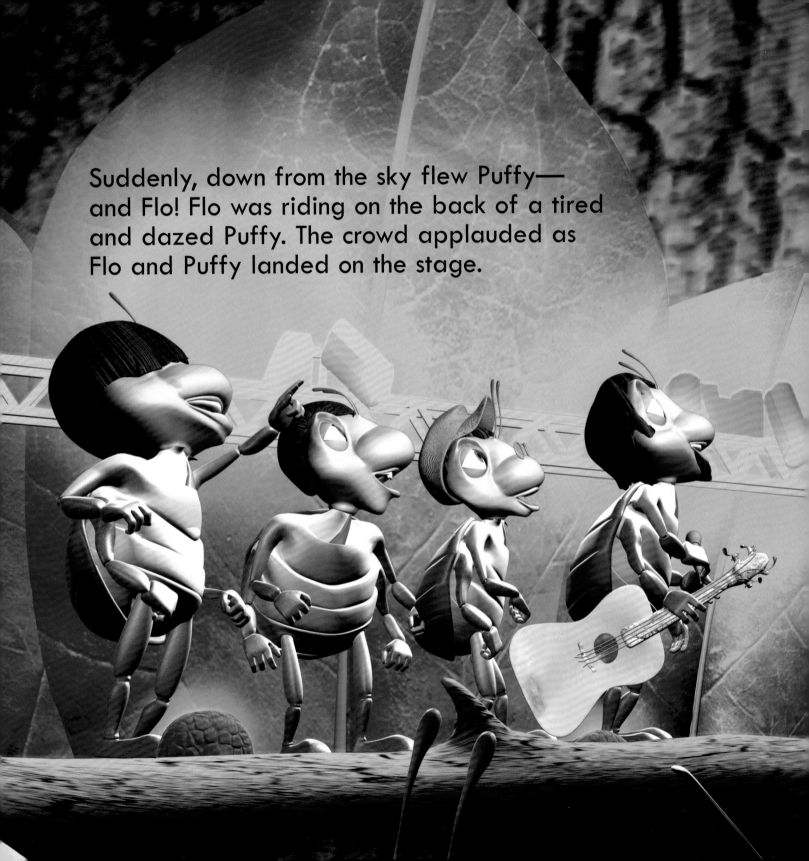

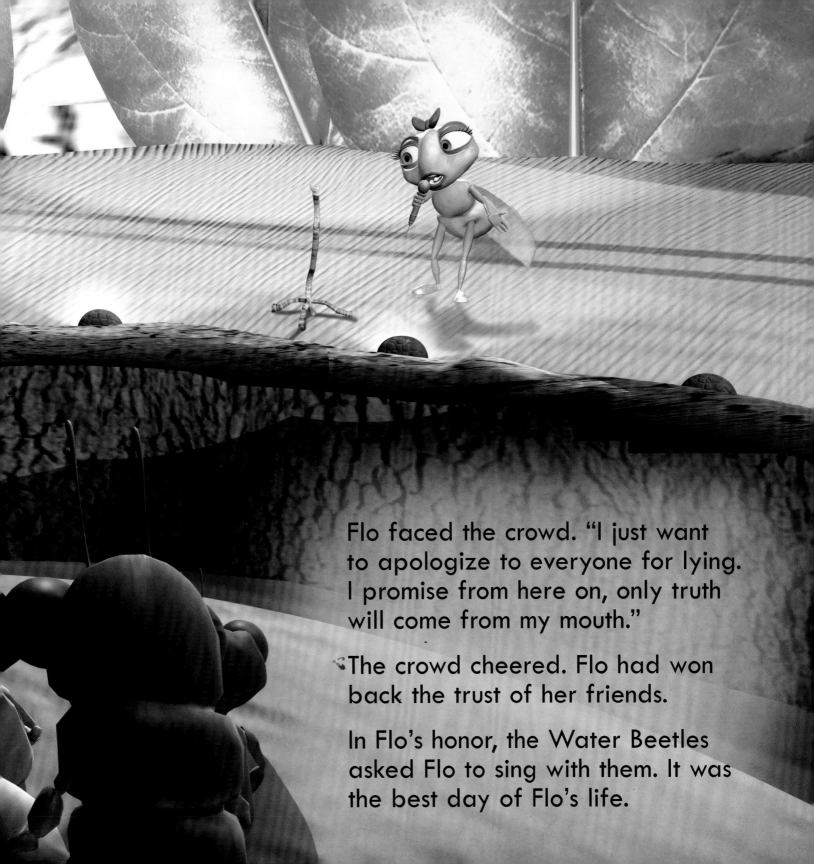

Flo faced the crowd. "I just want to apologize to everyone for lying. I promise from here on, only truth will come from my mouth."

The crowd cheered. Flo had won back the trust of her friends.

In Flo's honor, the Water Beetles asked Flo to sing with them. It was the best day of Flo's life.

"Thank you, God, for helping me learn to tell the truth."

God was proud of Flo. From now on she could be trusted. She would keep her promises. She would mean what she said. She would tell the truth.

WEBSTER

THE SCAREDY SPIDER

Webster, a young spider on holiday, had
just arrived in the garden. He didn't know
that spiders weren't welcome there.
Everyone was scared of spiders.

But Webster was a scaredy spider. He was afraid of almost every- thing: leaves, sticks, caves, lizards, bugs—even Hermie the caterpillar. Hermie was afraid of Webster, too.

"A SPIDER!" Hermie yelled.

"A CATERPILLAR!"
Webster yelled.

Once Hermie and Webster stopped screaming and started talking, they became friends.

"I'm not a scary spider. I'm a scaredy spider. I'm afraid of almost everything."

"I will help you to be brave," Hermie said. "Follow me! And you can meet my friends."

At Flo the fly's house, they also found Schneider Snail, Antonio Ant, and Wormie the caterpillar.

When Flo saw Webster, she flew away.

When Schneider saw Webster, he zoomed away.

When Antonio saw Webster, he ran away.

Only Wormie stayed.

Webster asked Wormie, "How did you get so brave?"

"I know God is with me," Wormie said.

"God can help you be brave, too," Hermie said. "Right, God?"

"That's right, Hermie," God said. "Webster, you are safe with Me. I'm always with you, even when you are afraid."

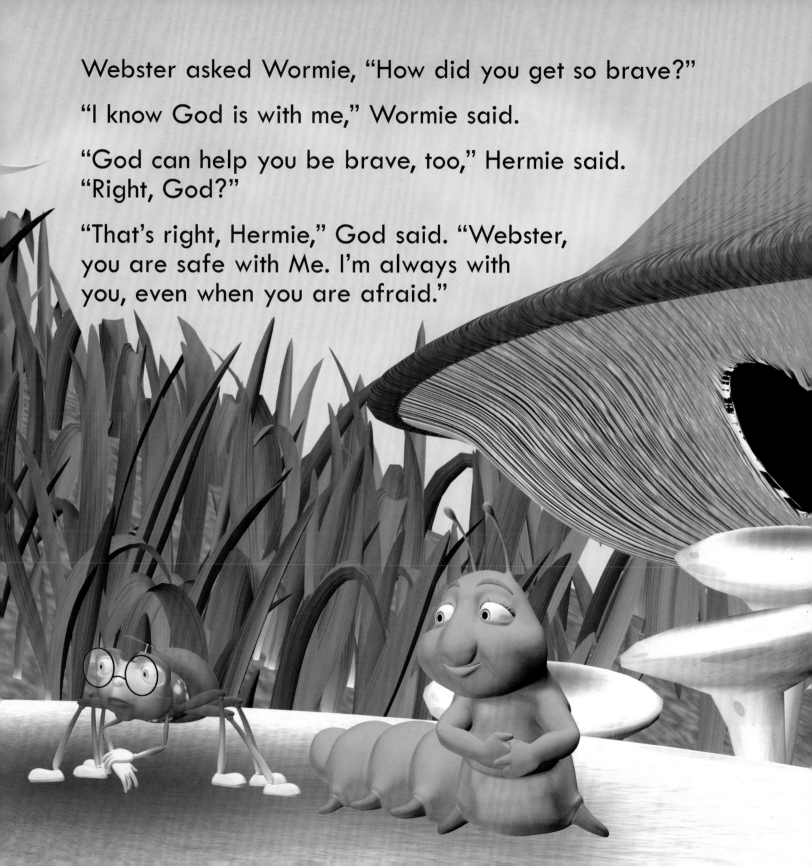

Webster was too scared to listen. He ran away.

"Webster's going to need a friend to remind him that I love him," God said.

"I'll be his friend," Hermie promised.

Hermie found Webster. "Let's dress you like a ladybug. No one's afraid of a ladybug."

Webster agreed. But it didn't work.

When the ladybugs saw Webster, they screamed, **"A SPIDER!"** and ran away.

"I've got it!" Hermie said. "Let's plan a big concert starring you. Everyone loves a concert."

But it didn't work.

When the crowd saw Webster, they shrieked, "A SPIDER!" and ran away.

The garden buzzed with news of the spider. Hermie and Wormie tried to convince the other bugs that Webster was a friendly spider, but no one listened.

"Webster has to leave!" they said.

As everyone talked, the ladybug twins came up with a plan of their own.

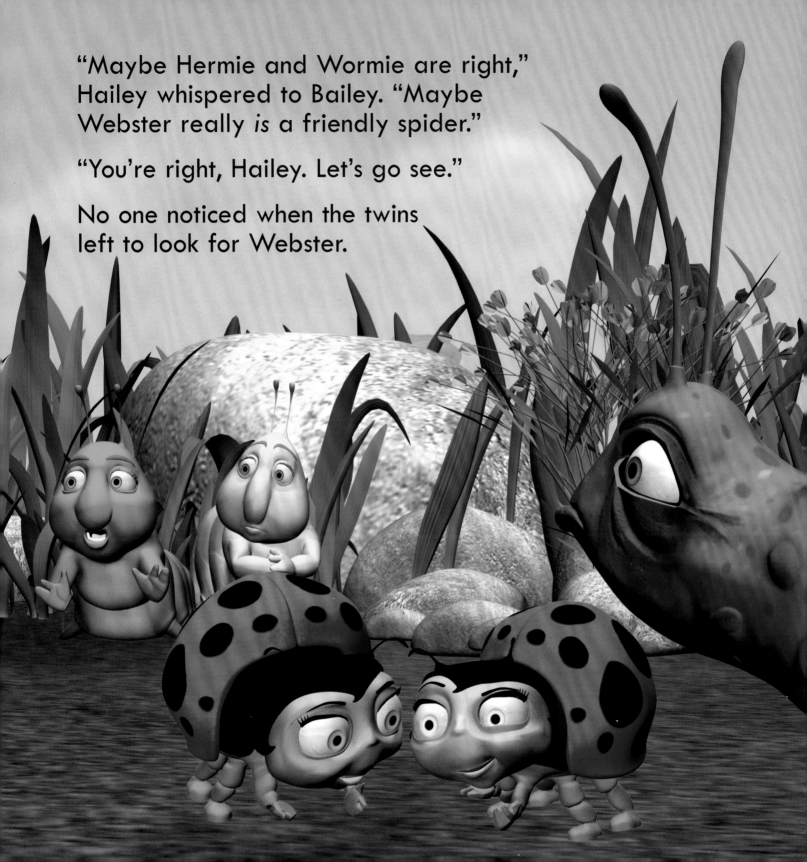

"Maybe Hermie and Wormie are right," Hailey whispered to Bailey. "Maybe Webster really *is* a friendly spider."

"You're right, Hailey. Let's go see."

No one noticed when the twins left to look for Webster.

As the crowd went to tell Webster to leave, Hermie and Wormie prayed.

"God, what can we do to help Webster?"

"Be his friend," God said. "The other bugs are scared of Webster. But because I am always with each of you, no one has to be afraid."

Hermie and Wormie were looking for Webster when they heard:

"MAMA, HELP US!"

Everyone rushed to the river.

It was Hailey and Bailey. The twins were on a runaway leaf in the river and headed straight for a dangerous waterfall.

"FLY, LADYBUGS, FLY!" Wormie said.

"We can't. We're stuck on this gooey, sticky leaf," said Hailey.

"SOMEBODY HELP US!" Bailey cried.

But no one could reach them. The leaf was moving too fast.

Webster wanted to help. He was afraid, but he was more afraid for the ladybugs.

"What can I do, God?"

"You can help them, Webster," God said.

"Me?"

"Yes. Don't worry. I'll be with you."

For the first time, Webster felt brave.

Quickly, Webster spun a silk net to catch the runaway leaf. Then, he swung and landed beside the twins. He pulled Hailey, then Bailey from the sticky goo, and the twins flew to safety.

But now Webster was stuck.
"OH, NO!" The crowd gasped as
the web broke. Webster plunged
over the waterfall.

"**LOOK!**" shouted Hailey and Bailey.

Swinging up from the waterfall was . . .

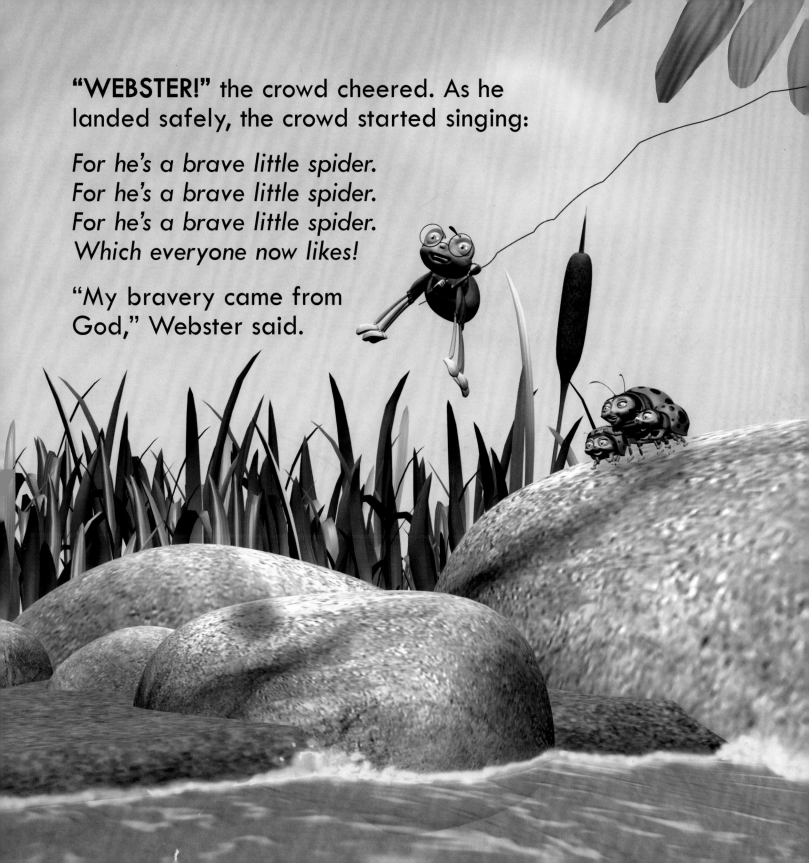

"**WEBSTER!**" the crowd cheered. As he landed safely, the crowd started singing:

For he's a brave little spider.
For he's a brave little spider.
For he's a brave little spider.
Which everyone now likes!

"My bravery came from God," Webster said.

"Thank You, God, for being with me today."

"Webster, I was with you every time you were afraid," God said. "I'm always with you."

From that day forward, Webster was no longer a scaredy spider. Soon he had many new friends. Whenever Webster was afraid, he remembered that God was with him. And that made Webster brave.

BUZBY
THE MISBEHAVING BEE

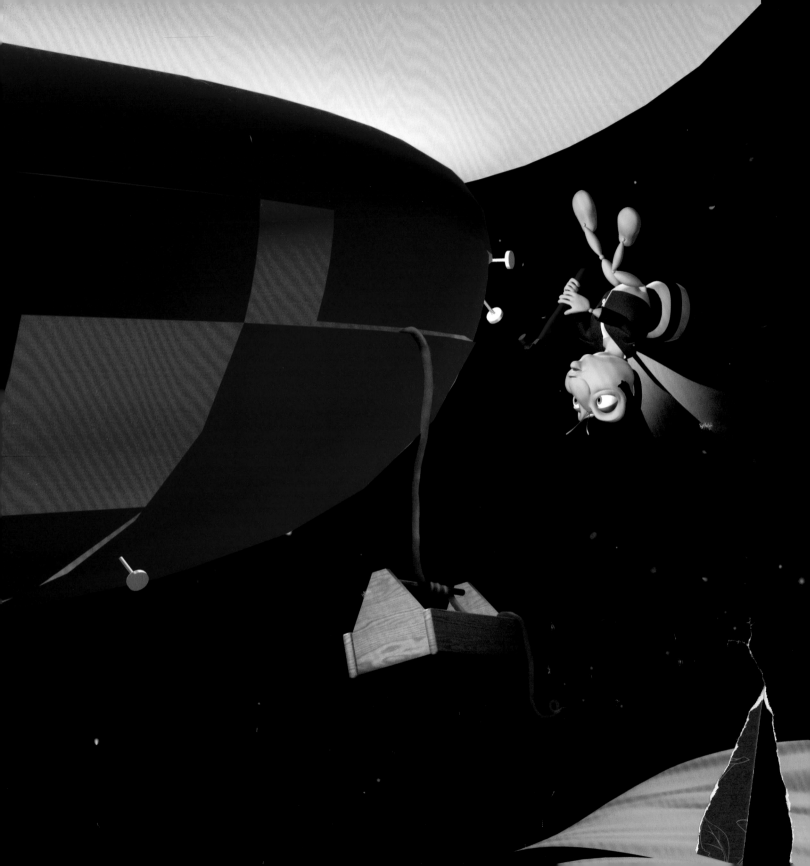

Buzby the misbehaving bee was always
breaking the rules. One night he made
so much noise working on his hive,
Hermie the caterpillar couldn't sleep.

Buzby didn't care. "I'm *king* of the bees,
and I'll do as I please."

And he did.

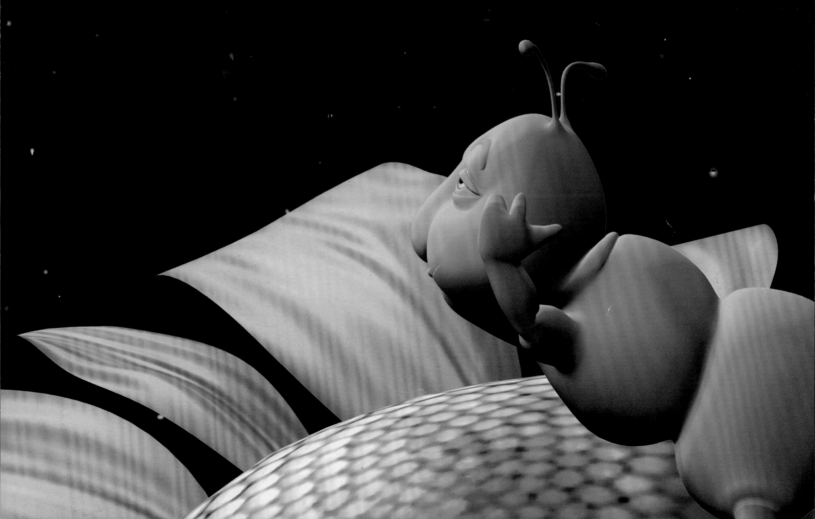

The next morning, Hermie and Wormie stood in the garden talking to Lucy Ladybug and her twins, Hailey and Bailey. Suddenly, Buzby buzzed by so fast that it turned Hermie, Wormie, and Lucy upside down! The twins laughed.

"Who is that?" Hailey asked.

"He's so cool." Bailey sighed.

Lucy Ladybug told her twins, "Stay away from that misbehaving Buzby." But the twins didn't listen.

THE GARDEN GOLDEN RULES

1. Always listen to God.
2. Don't open the gate!
3. Do listen to your parents.
4. Do help one another.
5. Do love one another.
6. Don't hurt another bug's feelings.
7. Don't make a mess.
8. Don't cause others to do wrong.
9. No speeding.
10. No loud noises after bedtime.

Hermie and Wormie decided to show Buzby the Garden Golden Rules.

Buzby shook his head. "I'm too cool for rules. I'm *king* of the bees, and I'll do as I please." And he left.

Buzby broke all of the Garden Golden Rules. He even dropped acorns on the ants' hill.

And all the while, Buzby said: "I'm too cool for rules! I'm *king* of the bees, and I'll do as I please."

And he did.

Hermie and Wormie prayed to God for help with Buzby.

God knew about Buzby. "I've known many like Buzby who don't like to follow the rules. Buzby doesn't understand that rules are to keep him and others safe. Rules are a way of saying, 'I love you.'"

God promised He would talk to Buzby.

Buzby took a sip of honey and smacked his lips. "I'm *king* of the bees. That's me."

Then he heard a voice call his name.

"Buzby."

"Who said that?" Buzby looked around "Who is talking to the *king* of the bees?"

"It's God, Buzby. I'm the *King of Everything*. You should follow the Garden Golden Rules."

But Buzby didn't want to listen to God. He flew away.

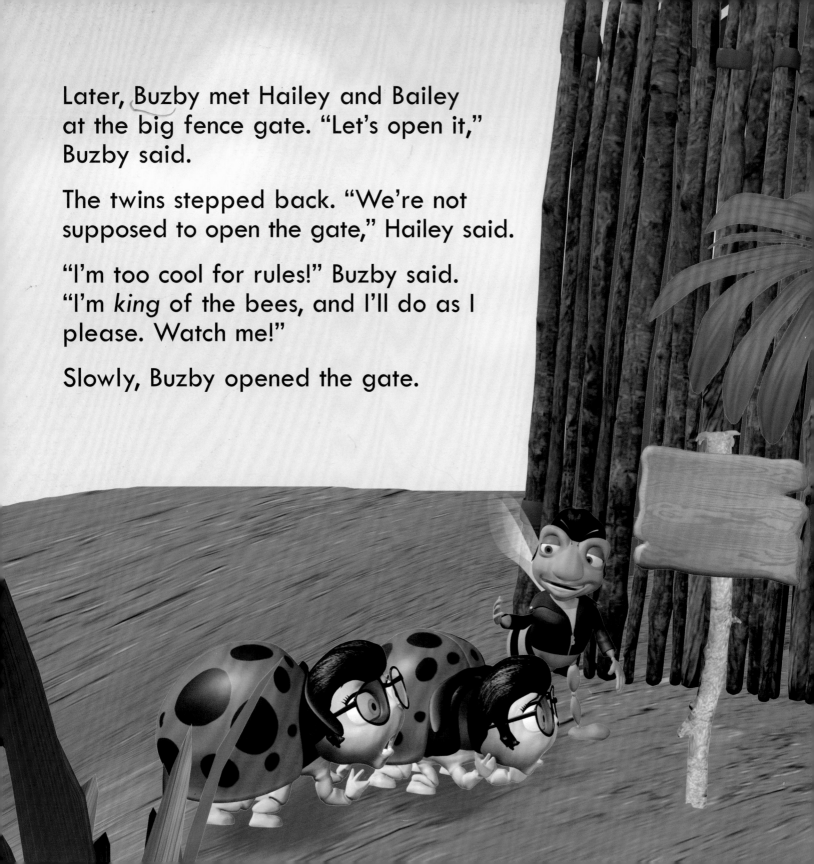

Later, Buzby met Hailey and Bailey at the big fence gate. "Let's open it," Buzby said.

The twins stepped back. "We're not supposed to open the gate," Hailey said.

"I'm too cool for rules!" Buzby said. "I'm *king* of the bees, and I'll do as I please. Watch me!"

Slowly, Buzby opened the gate.

First there was silence. Then a rumbling.
Then a shaking. Then a quaking.

Then, standing before Buzby, Hailey,
and Bailey was a BIG, BIG frog.

"Big Bully Croaker!" Hailey screamed.

"Run for your life!" Bailey shouted.

Quickly, Buzby and the twins
flew away.

The BIG frog hopped through the garden, smashing everything in his path.

"Oh, no! He broke my beehive." Buzby was sad.

"Buzby," God said.

But Buzby didn't want to listen to God. Buzby flew away.

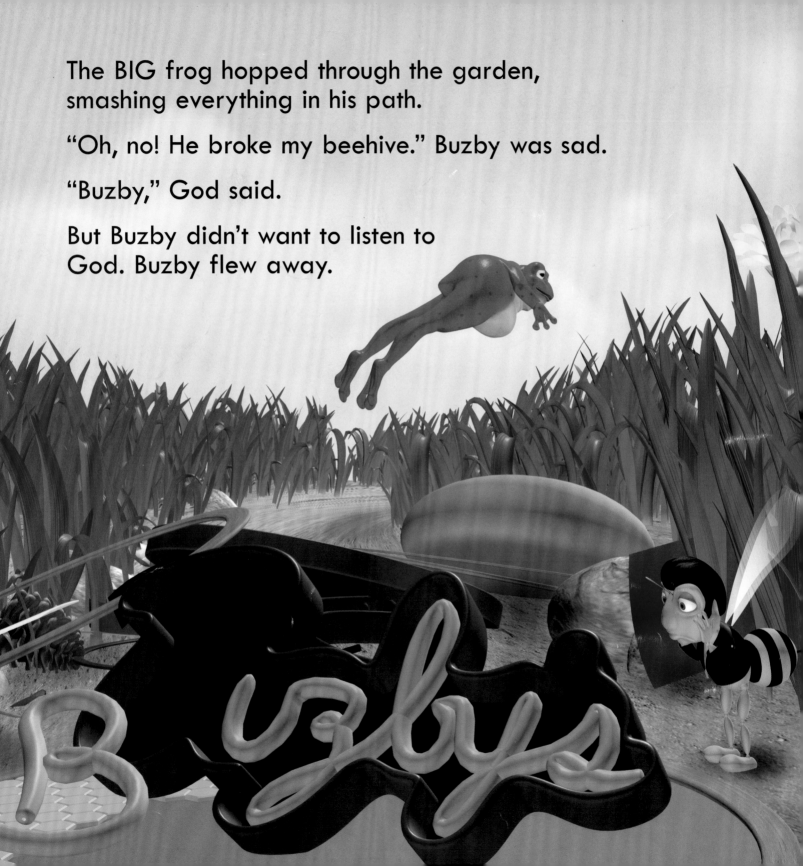

When the ants found Buzby's broken hive, they did what would please God and put it back together.

Meanwhile, other garden bugs had seen the open gate.

"Big Bully Croaker is on the loose!"

"Run for your lives!"

"Hurry, everyone! Go to the anthill. We'll be safe underground," Hermie said.

Just as the last bug made it safely inside, they heard . . .

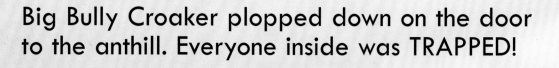

THUMP!

Big Bully Croaker plopped down on the door to the anthill. Everyone inside was TRAPPED!

When Buzby saw that the ants had fixed his hive, he felt bad about dropping acorns on their hill.

He prayed: "God, I'm sorry I broke the rules. I promise to obey them from now on. Will You forgive me?"

"Of course, Buzby," God said. "I love you. That's why I have rules to keep you safe."

Then God told Buzby to rescue the others. And this time Buzby listened.

Buzby flew toward the giant frog. Big Bully Croaker tried to grab Buzby with his tongue, but Buzby pointed his stinger at the frog.

"Let my friends go!" Buzby said.

Now, bees don't like frogs, but frogs
REALLY don't like angry bees.

Big Bully Croaker jumped off that anthill
and quickly hopped away.

Everyone thanked Buzby for rescuing them.
"Listen up," Buzby said. "I'm sorry I broke the garden rules.
Now I know that rules are cool. Will you forgive me?"